To my three most favorite people to make pancakes with: Miles, Hayden, and Dorothy —tf

To my son the chef, Drew —cf

Tyler Makes Pancakes!
Text copyright © 2012 by Tyler Florence
Illustrations copyright © 2012 by Craig Frazier
All rights reserved. Manufactured in China.
No part of this book may be used or reproduced in any manner whatsoever without written permission except in the case of brief quotations embodied in critical articles and reviews. For information address HarperCollins Children's Books, a division of HarperCollins Publishers, 10 East 53rd Street, New York, NY 10022.
www.harpercollinschildrens.com

Library of Congress Cataloging-in-Publication Data is available.
ISBN 978-0-06-204752-6

Typography by Craig Frazier
12 13 14 15 16   SCP   10 9 8 7 6 5 4 3 2 1

First Edition

Tyler
MAKES PANCAKES!

WRITTEN BY
Tyler Florence

ILLUSTRATED BY
Craig Frazier

HARPER
An Imprint of HarperCollins Publishers

"Tofu! I just had the coolest dream. There were pancakes in outer space and I was the captain of a pancake spaceship!" Tyler said. "Now I'm hungry and there's only one thing I want for breakfast!"

1. eggs
2. buttermilk
3. butter
4. flour
5. maple syrup

"You got it—pancakes! Let's surprise Mom and Dad. I've got my list ready. Let's hit the road and go to Mr. Jones's market."

"Morning, Mr. Jones," said Tyler. "I'm making pancakes. Can you help me find everything I need?"

"You bet, Tyler," said Mr. Jones. "I love pancakes, too. Come on in!"

"What do you need?" asked Mr. Jones.

"Eggs! Hey, there they are in the refrigerator," said Tyler.

"Yup," said Mr. Jones. "These just came in fresh."

"Fresh from what?" asked Tyler.

"From chickens!" said Mr. Jones.

"I don't see them....Where are they?" asked Tyler.

"Well, just imagine…

...that we are out on a farm."

"Cool," said Tyler. "Who's that?"

"That's Polly Petaluma. She's a star!
She lays the eggs you need for your
pancake batter, and they're the best!"

"Tofu, stop chasing that chicken!" said Tyler.

"What's next?" asked Mr. Jones.

"Buttermilk—whatever that is. Is it butter, or is it milk? Does it come from a butter cow?" asked Tyler.

"Nope. Buttermilk comes from regular cows," said Mr. Jones. "And guess what? There is no butter in buttermilk! It's just what's left over after you make butter. It's lemony and thicker and creamier than regular milk. It makes pancakes super fluffy and extra delicious. Looks like Tofu likes it."

"The next thing I need is flour," said Tyler. "I know what it looks like, but what is it? Does it come from some kind of flower?"

"No, but it *does* come from a plant," said Mr. Jones. "It's called wheat and it grows in flat places like Kansas. Big machines grind the wheat until it's a powder. Then you can use it in all kinds of baking, like honey bread, pizza, cupcakes...you name it!"

"Tofu! Get out of there!" said Tyler.
"There are no cupcakes inside that bag."

"Oooooh, look at these blueberries! My mom *loves* blueberries. Can I use them in pancakes?" Tyler asked.

"Blueberry pancakes are my extra-special favorites," said Mr. Jones. "Want to guess where blueberries come from?"

"Well, from here. The sign says the produce section," said Tyler.

"Well, you're right." Mr. Jones laughed. "But before that, blueberries are grown on bushes. You have to pick a lot to fill one of these little boxes."

"Hey, Tofu, we can't forget the most important thing—sticky, gooey maple syrup. Mmmmmmm," said Tyler. "Wow, look at all these bottles of syrup…. How do I know which one to get?"

"Only the best for your pancakes, Tyler, and that syrup comes from way up in Vermont," said Mr. Jones.

"Does it grow there?" asked Tyler.

"It doesn't exactly grow," said Mr. Jones. "Maple syrup comes from maple trees. In the cold, early spring, sap drains from the leaves and down the trunk. We tap a little pipe into the trunk and out drips raw maple syrup. But you can't eat it yet."

"Why not? Isn't it ready?" asked Tyler.

"Nope. You need to boil the raw syrup first, until it turns thick, golden brown, and super yummy."

"Now I'm *really* hungry," said Tyler, "and my list is done. Yay! Time to make the pancakes."

"Off you go. I put a little bit of bacon in your bag," said Mr. Jones. "It's great with pancakes. And here is a cantaloupe I just picked from my garden out back."

"Bye, Mr. Jones! Thanks for helping me.
Come on, Tofu, let's get cooking!" said Tyler.

"Okay, Tofu, here we go," said Tyler.

"Hi, Dad. You got up just in time to help me with breakfast," said Tyler. "You can hold the pan and I'll pour the batter!"

"I'll do anything for pancakes, Tyler," said Dad. "I hope we have syrup!"

"We have lots," said Tyler. "From Vermont!
And Mr. Jones gave us bacon and cantaloupe too."

"Now that's what I call breakfast!" said Dad.
"I'll get Mom."

"Here it comes!" said Tyler. "Let's eat!"

"I love breakfast," said Tyler, "and I love you! Next time I'm going to make dinner…. What do you think, Tofu? Don't tell me—spaghetti?"

TYLER'S
BLUEBERRY · BUTTERMILK
PANCAKES
RECIPE

Ingredients:
2 cups whole-wheat flour
¼ cup sugar
2 teaspoons baking soda
3 teaspoons baking powder
a pinch of salt
3 eggs
2 cups buttermilk
3 tablespoons melted butter
1 cup fresh blueberries

Directions:
In a large bowl, sift together the flour, sugar, baking
soda, baking powder, and salt. In another bowl, add the
eggs, buttermilk, and butter and mix well. Add the wet
ingredients together with the dry and whisk until well
blended. Fold in blueberries.

In a large nonstick skillet, melt an additional tablespoon
of butter over medium heat. Pour equal amounts of
batter to make 3 or 4 five-inch circles.

Cook the pancakes until bubbles rise from the middle of
each pancake.

Flip and cook for another 2 to 4 minutes. Keep cooked
pancakes in a warm oven as you cook off the remaining
batter.

Top with butter and Vermont maple syrup.

Makes about 16 to 20 pancakes.

Wheat is a type of grass that is grown all over the world. It is usually more than three feet tall! The kernels are taken from the stalk and are ground in a mill to make flour for baking. The best flour for taste and nutrition uses the whole kernel and is called whole-wheat flour.

3 ft.

Pure maple syrup is one of the sweetest things that nature makes. It tastes great, it's lower in calories than butter, and it has minerals and the good sugar that keeps your body moving when you're playing with your friends.

An adult hen can lay about one egg a day, maybe two. Eggs come in many different colors, but we mostly get white and brown eggs. Eggs are a super source of protein, which makes you strong and fast. Who came first—the chicken or the egg?

Did You Know?

It takes one gallon of milk to make half a pint of buttermilk. Buttermilk has less fat in it than regular milk. It contains lots of minerals, like potassium, phosphorus, and calcium, and nutrients, like vitamin B12.

Blueberries are a fabulous source of vitamin A and vitamin C, which are good for fighting colds and other diseases. Blueberries have the most anti-oxidants of any fruit. Antioxidants are super good for our heart and other parts of our bodies. Yummy.